Hi, diary . . .

Everything is new today or supposed to be. I went to bed twelve years old and woke up thirteen, a teen-ager. I thought about staying up all night, but I fell asleep like any other night.

I don't know what I expected but everyone has been saying, "Wait till you're older, then you'll understand, then you can do this or you can do that . . ." But when are you older? I bet I'll be a little old lady hobbling around and they'll still say, "Wait till you're older." Frankly, for a lot of things I can wait. I don't think being a teen-ager is so great, although this is only the first day. Maybe it gets better. . . .

Nobody Has to Be a Kid Forever

a Kid Forever

by Hila Colman

AN ARCHWAY PAPERBACK
POCKET BOOKS . NEW YORK

POCKET BOOKS, a Simon & Schuster division of
GULF & WESTERN CORPORATION
1230 Avenue of the Americas, New York, N.Y. 10020

Copyright © 1976 by Hila Colman

Published by arrangement with Crown Publishers, Inc.
Library of Congress Catalog Card Number: 75-25810

ISBN: 0-671-29926-3

First Pocket Books printing April, 1977

2nd printing

Trademarks registered in the United States and other countries.

Printed in the U.S.A.

For Joyce

Nobody Has to Be
a Kid Forever

September

Hi, diary, everything is new today or supposed to be. I went to bed twelve years old and woke up thirteen, a teen-ager. I thought about staying up all night, but I fell asleep like any other night.

I don't know what I expected but everyone has been saying, "Wait till you're older, then you'll understand, then you can do this or you can do that . . ." But when are you older? I bet I'll be a little old lady hobbling around and they'll still say, "Wait till you're older." Frankly, for a lot of things I can wait. I don't think being a teen-ager is so great, although this is only the first day. Maybe it gets better. On the other hand, my

1

sister Didi has been a teen-ager for years and it sure hasn't helped her any. The only difference I can see is that she washes her hair every day instead of once a week the way normal people do, and she gets off the phone only to go to the john.

My mother didn't look so happy when she came in to wish me a happy birthday. As a matter of fact she hasn't been looking happy at all lately, and neither has my father. They don't scream at each other; instead, my mother snaps at my father and my father sulks. She bangs pots around in the kitchen and says, "Damn it I hate housework," and my father says, "No one's life is perfect," and starts sulking. I don't know what they expect of me. I have a pile of homework to do so I don't see why I should do the dishes. And when I do offer to help, my mother throws dirty looks at my father and says, "I don't want my daughters to grow up to be household drudges." My father pretends to be reading the paper, but then he'll mutter, "These damn women think men have it so easy . . ."

After my mother kissed me happy birthday, and tried to look cheerful, she said, "You're a woman now, Sarah, darling. Except," and she gave a sad sigh, "it's not so simple. Being a woman can be lousy. You spend your life bring-

2

ing up your kids, taking your husband's shirts to the laundry and then suddenly one day you wake up and you're old and you have nothing. Absolutely nothing."

"You have me, don't you?" What a birthday greeting! First she tells me "You're a woman," and then she tells me what a disaster it is.

"Yes of course, darling, I do have you." She became all soft and apologetic. "I shouldn't be talking to you this way. What would you like to do today? I thought we could go out together, just you and me, and have some fun. Do something interesting."

Then I felt awful because I had planned to have lunch and spend the afternoon with my grandmother. The truth is that I really get along better with my grandmother than with my mother, and we have more fun. It's a terrible thing to say, I know, but my mother—well, she's my mother, and I always have the feeling that she expects me to be something I'm not. She says she doesn't like to pry but then she'll ask funny questions to find out if I'm popular in school, or she'll say, "you don't have to always wear turtle neck sweaters." She wants me to be pretty and popular and get all A's. With my grandmother I can be me, plain Sarah Grinnell.

My mother looked sad when I told her Grandma had invited me for lunch, and I felt awful. I know she wanted me to invite her to come along, but that would have ruined everything. I suppose I'm selfish, but hell, it was my birthday. "Why don't you do something with Dad today?" I said. (It was Saturday and he was home.)

"He's still sleeping. He already announced that he was very tired and wanted to just rest today." She said it as if he was committing a crime.

There was no point in suggesting Didi. She's never home, so it ended up with my feeling a creep when I left for Grandma's.

Grandma was playing a Louis Armstrong record when I got there. She likes what she calls old-fashioned jazz, and she's getting me to like it too. She's really dynamite—she showed me how to do the Charleston. She's in her sixties and she doesn't try to look young, she just is. She never says things like, "let's have some fun," but she has plans. We went way down to Southport where old houses are being restored and there are old boats to go on, and funny streets, and she took me to a restaurant with sawdust on the floor and I stuffed myself with fried clams.

I didn't want to talk about my parents, but after all my mother is her daughter so I thought it was okay. I told her that something was brewing at home and that it made me nervous.

She didn't give me the old bull that everything was going to be all right. She said, "I'm worried, too. Your mother is going through some kind of phase that is making her unhappy. I think it was a mistake for her to have given up her music career when she married your father, but she did it, and now I'm afraid she is bored and unhappy. Your father, too, is unhappy. He wanted to be a painter, but he had to make money when you girls came along so he became a textile designer. I think they're both disappointed with their lives."

"Then they shouldn't have had us. I'm never going to have kids if they spoil your life."

"It doesn't have to be that way. Young people today are different. They don't believe that they have to give their kids the best of everything. They get along on less, and try to do what they want to do."

"I never asked them to make a lot of money." But then I thought of how much I'd wanted a new hi-fi set for my birthday, which I got, and I felt like a creep.

"Maybe I should give back my new hi-fi set?" I said, quaking that my grandmother was going to say yes.

It was a relief when she shook her head. "That

would be silly. It's a whole way of life, and, Sarah, none of it is your fault. Remember that."
- Famous last words. It's depressing to have my mother look weepy and my father gloomy, which happens a hell of a lot of the time these days.

September

I thought now that Didi and I were both teen-
agers we could be friends. That was stupid. I
don't know why she is so mean to me. There I
was last night with a nervous stomach on account
of having to go to that new school in the morning,
when she starts telling me how lousy it is. "Whatever made you pick that school?" she said, as if
she hadn't known about it for months already.
"It's got all the drips in New York in it, kids who
couldn't get in any other place. You'll never get
to college from that dump."

"Who said I wanted to go to college?"

"You're supposed to be the brain in the family."

7

"Knock it off. I don't see anything so great about your Academy of Drama or whatever you call it. The boys are a bunch of queers."

"That's not true," she yelled. "Just because men act and dance doesn't make them queers."

"You ought to know," I said. "Anyway, leave me alone. I'm meditating."

"You're what?"

"You heard me. I'm meditating."

She gave me a dirty look. "You're nuts. You look sick. Are you going to upchuck?"

"I will if you don't get out of here," I screamed.

I don't really know very much about transcendental meditation, only what my friend Millie has told me. Her mother's into it, and she's taken Millie to her teacher. Millie has a mantra, a word she was given, but she won't tell me what it is. She says it's her own word and her own secret. She says it helps her not to be so uptight and worried, and she has plenty to worry about. Even more than I. She has no father, at least nowhere in sight, and her mother's always going off someplace to make a movie or go on a trip with her boyfriend, and leaving Millie with that dopey neighbor Millie hates. I hope TM helps Millie, but I think a family, even a gloomy one, might be better.

September

First day of school. I always thought that if I worried about something enough it couldn't possibly turn out to be as bad as I expected. I was wrong. Dead wrong. That school is a mess. Everyone was wandering around, no one knew where they belonged—one girl, Kathy Stickney, and I were sent to three different rooms before we landed in the right one. We laughed so hard we were almost sent out of that one. Kathy may turn out to be a friend. She's kind of pretty, she has a friendly smile and eyes that sometimes look scared, which I can sympathize with because she probably is scared. She told me she lost twenty pounds over the summer and I thought she was suggesting I could do the same, but she quickly said, "Oh no, you look terrific. I just wanted you to know because I'm not used to the new me yet." We didn't have time to pursue that further, but it sounded interesting.

I'm going to this school because Millie and I got scholarships to it—Millie because of her art and me because of my writing. It's that kind of a school; they want "creative" kids. My father was dead set against it. He said, "She won't learn a damn thing in a place like that, she's got plenty of time to be creative, but right now she ought to learn some math and history, and how to write a simple English sentence." My mother talked him down. They had quite a row about it. Mom said it was more important for a woman to have a professional career than to waste time learning a lot of stuff she was never going to use. "Not that they don't have a fine academic curriculum there," Mom said, "but they'll take her writing seriously, and that's what counts." Mom is pretty mixed up: she's so into the woman's thing, yet she still believes the sciences are for men and the arts are for women. She's like an old-fashioned lady dressed up in modern clothes.

She scares me because I'm not that sure I want to be a writer. I haven't had much time yet to think about something else. Who knows, maybe I'll want to be a veterinarian, or a truck driver or a biochemist. There are a lot of things a person can be.

Parents are peculiar. If a kid wants to be something—like my friend Howard, who wants to be a forest ranger—the parents are always dead set against it. But if you don't know for sure what you want to be, then they decide what you want to be. Either way you lose.

I met Millie after school and that was pretty peculiar. We never see each other much over the summer because we go up to our house in Truro on Cape Cod and Millie stays in the city (which she pretends to like but I'm not sure she does). She sure changed this summer. She was wearing a long skirt and lots of eye makeup, and while she agreed that the school stinks, I don't think she meant it. You can't really talk to someone you think isn't leveling with you, and Millie and I had always been straight with each other. We went to have a soda but she seemed nervous and fidgety, and kept looking at the clock on the wall.

"Do you have to be someplace?" I asked her.

She looked embarrassed. "As a matter of fact, yes. This neat boy Roger asked me to meet him at a coffee shop on 87th Street."

I couldn't believe it. "I thought you and I had a date."

"I didn't think you'd mind . . . I . . ."

"Isn't a girl date as important as a boy date?" Millie giggled. "Well, it isn't, is it? I mean if

11

you had a date with a boy I'd understand. We could have an agreement. Any time either one of us got a date with a boy that would come first. Don't you think that's a good idea?"

"It's a terrible idea. A person is a person. Why couldn't you have made a date with Roger for to-morrow? Who is Roger, anyway?"

"He's a boy in my drawing class. With long, curly black hair. He was going to tell me where to buy paints."

I roared. I couldn't help it. "Millie, you've been buying paints for four years! All right, go off and meet your curly-haired friend." I got up and picked up the check. She fumbled with her purse, but I was faster. "Be my guest," I snapped.

I was furious when I left her, but sad and hurt too. I had been counting on Millie—she was one of the reasons I had agreed to the school, and now she was deserting me for BOYS. I felt as if I'd lost my last friend, and I had. I felt like crying but I wasn't going to give in. I concentrated on thinking that Roger was the biggest creep in the world.

But that wasn't much comfort, because I couldn't help but wonder what was wrong with me, why I didn't have a boyfriend, why I didn't even care about boys. I tried to think about being a great and famous writer and how I'd put Millie in a book and show how boy crazy she was. But that didn't help either because I thought about Millie being hurt, and that made me feel sorry for her instead of angry. My English teacher said that if I want to be a writer I have to be objective about people but I don't want to be a cold fish. He says I'm too intense and that I take everything too hard, but hell, if you don't *feel* things you may as well be a wet noodle.

Later

My family is wild, they really are. No one can put it together, they all go off in different directions and you never know what to expect. Sometimes I like the fact that they're not just ordinary people, but sometimes it gets on my nerves. My parents wanted to know how I liked the new school (of course) and were furious that I had nothing to say. "What about your teachers? Are they nice, do you like them?" Mom asked.

"How should I know? I hardly met them."

"You can tell. You're not talking, I can see."

"I've got nothing to say. There was nothing but confusion today."

"I hope *you're* not confused," my father said.

"Both the school and we expect a lot from you, Sarah. You know they don't hand out scholarships for nothing. You have an obligation to get everything you possibly can out of the privilege of going to a school like that."

I gave him a dirty look. "I had the impression you didn't think so much of that school."

"Don't be snotty. I raised some questions that I wanted answered, that's all."

It was useless to remind him that he'd had a big row with Mom about the school. Speaking of short and convenient memories . . .

Later in the evening, Dad gave me a pep talk. For a man who's supposed to believe in doing your own thing (although he certainly doesn't—he keeps saying he wants to paint but he never does, not even on weekends), he can hand out the platitudes like he made them up. "Sarah, you only get out of a school what you put into it, and if you start out thinking you know more than your teachers you'll get no place. You have a lot to learn, and the only way to learn is to keep your mind open. You're a bright girl but sometimes you can be too smart-ass for your own good. Don't forget that your scholarship isn't paying for all of it—it's costing us money to send you to that school and we expect you to make the most of it." Blah, blah, blah.

I went into my room, and sat by the window looking down at Central Park, but how can you think with a sister in the next room rehearsing lines at the top of her voice for a dumb Joan of Arc play they're doing at her school? The only thing that girl can see is her own name up in lights, DEIRDRE GRINNELL, Starring in . . .

This all sounds as if I don't love my family, and I honestly do. But sometimes it's hard.

October

It's a delicate problem that I have, and what to do I do not know. (A peculiar sentence, but when you feel peculiar it comes out peculiar.) It goes like this: Millie is suddenly very clingy; she wants to meet me every afternoon after school, but it isn't me that she's interested in, she only wants someone to talk to about Roger. "He's so sweet and shy," she says to me. "I know he's got a real thing about me, but he doesn't know how to express it. I give him all kinds of openings, but he doesn't know how to take them. He's so sweet . . . saves a seat next to him in art class, and helps me with my paints and easel, and at lunch we always go for a Coke or something, and when I don't meet you he walks me to the subway after school. I asked him to come down to the house with me but he got a funny look on his face, like he was scared, and said maybe some other time. What do you think?"

She was leaning with her elbows on the table looking at me as if I were a shrink. Millie is so sophisticated but sometimes she thinks I have all the answers, like somebody's mother—although mothers never give you any answers. (Mother knows best is about the dumbest idea anyone ever had.)

Millie's a problem. We used to be close friends, but now we're drifting apart. Sometimes I really don't like her all that much, but I feel sorry for her. She has a lousy time being alone so much, so I feel sorry for her and want to be nice to her. But I have a better time with Kathy Stickney. I don't know her very well, but when we are together we laugh a lot. She has a terrific sense of humor and a wild imagination. The other day we were riding on a Madison Avenue bus and she suddenly started talking to me in French. Then she went up to the bus driver and asked him directions in French, and the poor guy got so bewildered I was afraid he was going to hit a truck. She had me in hysterics. When we got off the bus she waved "au revoir" to everyone and they waved back.

To get back to Millie. It's awful to feel that

someone counts on you, but you no longer count on them, nor want to be counted on that much. Sometimes I feel the same way about my mother. I feel weighted down when she wants me to do things with her and acts as if she needs me a lot. I suppose it's unfair because I need her, but then she is my mother, and a kid needs a mother.

The peculiar part is that everything Millie says about Roger (except walking her to the subway because I don't take a subway) he does for me. I don't get it. She knows he's in my math and my English classes, but she doesn't know he saves a seat for me, and that he brought me a beautiful leather-bound copy of Keats's poems to read. He helps me with my math (my worst subject) and even calls me up at home at night to discuss our assignments. He acts sincere, but he's either a two-timer or boy scout who wants to "help people."

So there I sit listening to Millie describe in detail everything this boy scout or two-timer does for her that he does for me and she takes it all so seriously. So what do I do? Do I tell her? No, I can't, I've wanted to but I haven't been able to— she'll think I'm trying to take him away from her or she won't believe me. Then I think, forget it, it's none of my business if Roger Atkins wants to be nice to a dozen girls; that's his problem. But one of them shouldn't be Millie. If a boy smiles at her, she thinks he's crazy about her.

So I sit there like a dope and say, "Yes, Roger seems very nice, he's very polite," and I hope maybe she'll realize that a boy can be nice to you without its being a big deal, but Millie isn't interested in anything I say, she just wants an ear for her own voice.

October

The plot thickens. Roger asked me to spend Saturday afternoon with him. He wasn't at all shy or stammery about it. Came right out and said, "If you're not doing anything Saturday, you want to do something with me? We could go to a museum or for a walk or something." He really has a nice smile, and he is very smart in math, so right away I said, "That sounds great. I'd love it."

It was only when I met Millie after school that I felt like a creep. I couldn't even look her straight in the eye without my stomach going into a nose dive. Then she asked me what I was doing on Saturday and did I want to come down to the

Village (where she lives) and walk around with her, and I thought this is too much. I knew on my birthday that being a teen-ager was no fun, but I didn't think it would be this confusing.

People give me a great pain when they think that being a teen-ager is all fun and no headaches. They should know the problems we have, they may think they're not important, but believe me when you have the worries that I have it's no joke. Like an idiot I decided to ask my big, sophisticated sister what to do. What a mistake that was. "Don't be a jerk," she said. "Of course go out with what's his name—Roger—it's everyone for himself. What did Millie ever do for you? You don't owe her a damn thing. If he likes you better that's her problem, not yours."

Her advice only got me mad. She made everything sound worse, like I'd be a real rat if I did what she said. I don't want to follow in her footsteps—and if I had any doubts on that score I lost them when her boyfriend came down from his college near Boston. Not Harvard—he couldn't make it there as a janitor. He's the one she met on her trip to Europe and that she's crazy about. She may even be dumb enough to marry him.

Saturday is coming closer and closer and I still haven't told Millie. When I see her in school I try to avoid her, which is stupid.

Friday night

I did it. I went to have a Coke with Millie after
school and I told her Roger had asked me to
spend Saturday afternoon with him. That girl
ought to be an actress. It took her about one
minute to recover from the shock and then she
blinked her eyes and said, "Oh, are you going out
with that creep? I suppose everyone has to try
him once—he's been playing up to every girl in
school, so I guess it's your turn now."

She really had me fooled at first. I said, "I
thought you liked him so much. You've sat right
here raving about him."

"Oh, no, I caught on to him fast. He's sad the

way he tries so hard to get a girl. When did he ask you?"

"I don't remember." Then there was something in her face that gave the whole thing away, and it suddenly made sense. He had turned her down for Saturday and that's when she asked me . . . it made me feel awful. I thought of Millie all by herself in that crummy apartment of hers with her mother off someplace not even leaving anything in the house to eat, and I wanted to die.

But Millie's not the kind who wants you to feel sorry for her, not for a minute, although you do anyway. She pulled her face together and said, "I'm glad you're not counting on me for Saturday. Since you hadn't said anything, I made other plans." You've got to hand it to that girl, she can put up a front like no one else in the world. She's got guts. I tried to believe she wasn't lying, but I knew she was, and I almost said, "To hell with Roger, let's do something together." But then that would be calling her bluff, and I decided that would be mean.

Sunday

Something has happened to me. I don't even know how to explain what it is. The thing is, I always felt that going out with a boy was no different from going with a girl—of course I know they *are* different, but I meant that a friend is a friend. At least that's the way I always felt about Howard, who was a real friend to me when we were both going to the same school. I haven't seen him in ages but I think it would be the same now. But I felt *different* with Roger. He makes me feel aware of myself—the way he looks at me, and when we were walking, he took my hand and I felt a peculiar closeness, as if there was just the two of us.

I don't know if he felt the same or felt any of the things that I felt. I tried to remind myself of the things that Millie had said about him, about making a play for all the girls, but when he looked at me the way he did I couldn't believe it. No one could be that good a faker. We had a wonderful afternoon. We didn't do anything, we just walked around and then went for a soda. We didn't even talk that much, just walked, holding hands. It was perfect.

When I got home my mother said, "What did you do? You're glowing."

"She's got a boyfriend," Didi said.

"Shut up," I said, but I didn't feel as annoyed inside as I did when she used to make cracks about Howard. I wonder what that means?

Anyway, whatever it means, it was nice. When I sat down to do my math all I thought about was Roger. He is good looking and while I know looks aren't everything, it does make you feel good to be with someone you like looking at. He even made me feel good looking, not just plain Sarah Grinnell. I even thought about buying a dress, and then I got scared—I don't want to turn into a drip (like Didi), acting silly about boys and fussing with my hair and putting gook around my eyes and worrying all the time about whether someone's going to call me or not. I *hate* that stuff.

Almost November

I can't stand the way time goes by. I've been too busy to write or do anything. It suddenly hit me that a lot has been happening right here in this house, and I haven't been paying attention. My grandmother says it's my age—that it's okay for me to be self-absorbed because I'm discovering a lot of things about myself and that that's part of growing. But heck, I don't want to be one of those selfish egocentric people—I think of them as spending their lives picking blackheads out of their noses and not seeing anything else. But I am discovering interesting things about myself: My boobs are getting bigger, and I don't mind. As a matter of fact I sometimes get wild fantasies, like I wish there'd be a fire at school, or some accident (of course with no one getting hurt) just when I'm getting undressed for gym, and I'd have to run out without any clothes on, and Roger would see that I have a nice body. I don't have heavy thighs the way Kathy does, or hair on my belly like Millie is getting. I actually like to look at myself in the mirror when I come out of the shower or tub.

But here I am sounding off about myself, when I am really worried about my family. It's falling apart: everyone seems to be going off in different directions so that there isn't any *family* any more. We hardly ever have dinners together and I hate that.

Didi is always rehearsing for something at her idiot school or up in Boston weekends with her precious Eric. Last weekend she borrowed my best sweater and hasn't brought it back yet. "Don't worry, you'll get it back," she said, but I do worry because I think she lost it. I was a fool to lend it to her. The trouble with me is I keep thinking that if I'm nice to her, we'll be friends. But it never happens. My grandmother says, "Stop trying to hang on to Didi. You don't need her. It's nice if a sister is a friend, but being a sister doesn't make it so." I suppose she's right, but that doesn't stop me from still wanting a big sister who adores me. Fat chance with Didi, who will probably never adore anyone but herself.

My mother is now going to a consciousness-raising group that meets at seven o'clock which is when we always had dinner when we were an ordinary family. As far as I can see, the only thing that's been raised is a lot more hell. My father is furious and says it's barbaric to have meetings at seven o'clock. "If you have to do something so idiotic, why can't you meet at a civilized hour?" he demands almost every night when he comes home just as my mother is going out (three times a week).

"I have served you dinner for twenty years," my mother tells him, "and it's high time you served yourself." She slams the door behind her and my father mutters, "Those damn women picked this time on purpose."

So it's Dad and me eating some pukey frozen stuff, most of which we throw away. We stuff ourselves with cheese and crackers and peanuts while Dad watches the news and has a couple of drinks. I wouldn't mind eating with Dad if we had good food and he wasn't so preoccupied. But he looks sad. Sometimes he talks a little about how he wanted to be a painter instead of a textile designer, and he always ends up saying, "It's too late now." It's a terrible thing to say about one's own father, but I think he's scared—he acts as if his life was over and he's given up. Mom is unhappy, but at least she's trying to do something about it; Dad just mopes.

Our dinner conversation goes like this: "How is school, honey?"

"Okay."

Long silence.

"How is business going?" I ask, trying to be funny.

"Not so hot. I don't know what's going to happen. Business is lousy." Now it sounds as if he's worried about losing his job. That's all we need. I can't stand everything being so uncertain. On the news there was a story about a woman beating her child to death, and it suddenly occurred to me that not all parents love their children. I'm not even sure mine do now.

I went to see Grandma, and she was all excited about money being spent on defense, mirv-missiles and all that stuff, when people don't have jobs and are going hungry. But I said, "I have too many problems to think about things like that. I can't do anything about it, anyway."

"You will when you're older," Grandma said. "But even now, if you open up your mind to the rest of the world you'll see your own problems in a better perspective. Everything isn't black or white. Life is problems, there are always problems."

"I'm sick of mine. I'm scared," I told her. It was hard to explain what I meant. I was scared of not being sure of anyone, even my own parents. I mean parents were supposed to be there when you needed them—to tell you to do your homework and read a story that you wrote, to remember to give you lunch money or buy a pair of shoes or even to yell or be yelled at. Parents are often a pain but they're a necessity.

"Lots of kids all over the world are growing up without parents," Grandma said. "Telling you about the Vietnamese orphans isn't going to do you any good. But you're growing up, and your parents are having problems, so you are getting less attention. But that doesn't mean they don't love you. In the end you have to count on yourself."

Grandma is always very sensible, but she doesn't know that counting on myself is like counting on a canoe to cross the Atlantic.

November

Yesterday when I came home from school Mom said she wanted to talk to me. She sounded like she was going to tell me someone died.

"You're growing up so fast I hardly know you anymore," she said right off.

"I'm around." I meant that for a dig but it went right past her.

"Yes, I know. That's partly what I want to talk to you about."

"You mean you don't want me around?"

"Don't be silly, it's more that I don't want to be around . . ." She gave an uncertain laugh, and a deep sigh. "You're going to have to know sooner or later, so there's no sense in beating around

33

the bush. It's that I think I want to leave home for a while. It isn't that I don't love you and Didi, and Dad. . . . I love all three of you very much. But none of you really needs me anymore, and I feel that I'm wasting my own life. I haven't been much good to anyone lately . . . and, well, the truth is I feel more alive, more myself, when I'm out of this house, doing things on my own for myself. It's hard to explain, and I suppose I sound very selfish, and maybe I am . . ."

I didn't know what to say, and I didn't know what she wanted me to say. The funny thing was that after she said it, I realized that I had known she was going to say that. I mean I wasn't surprised.

"You mean you're going to live someplace else? Have you got an apartment?"

She looked hurt. "You seem in a hurry to get rid of me. I said I was just thinking about leaving. . . . I haven't *done* anything about it."

"Does Dad know?"

"He knows I've been thinking about it. I haven't said anything definite and won't until I've made all the arrangements. I couldn't stand another big discussion. When I'm ready to leave he'll know. I think that's the wisest, don't you?"

As if she was asking *me* for advice! But she wasn't, she wanted someone, even me, to say, you've got a great idea, Mom! Terrific! But I didn't think it was terrific. I thought what does she want me to do about it, and oh, God, why does this have to happen to me? And I thought of the stupidest thing in the whole world: who's going to iron my blouses? She does them so much better than me. Selfish, mean thoughts! I wanted desperately to be grown up, but I felt more like crying than anything. I wanted to say something wise, but instead I yelled, "How should I know what you should do? Don't ask me!"

She looked pale and shaken. "I thought you would understand," she said. Then she rambled on about how I would have to take more responsibility in the house, that Virginia would still come in once a week to do the cleaning, but in between times I'd have to manage, that she was counting on me since Didi was home so little . . . blah, blah.

I didn't want to hear any of it. "We'll figure things out," I mumbled. I didn't know what I felt. I felt sorry for her, sorry for myself and sorry for Dad. I also felt angry. Angry that she was disrupting my life without my truly understanding why. That's the trouble with grown-ups. They give you half-truths. They never really level with you. How could she expect me to understand what I didn't know?

"I've got a lot of homework to do," I said, and I marched into my room. Then I burst into tears. I was crying because I was angry, at least in the beginning. But then my mind, like it had a will of its own, started thinking all the things I hadn't wanted to say to Mom: please don't go away, please, please stay here and love Daddy and Didi and me—why do you want to go away if you love us?

Day after Thanksgiving

God, I wish I knew what was going on. I love mysteries in books but not in real life. I hate them in this house. Mom's never said another word about what she told me, and we had Thanksgiving the way we always have, except I *felt* it was different. On the outside everything was the same, Mom cooked the turkey and Grandma brought pies, and even Didi stayed home for a change. But Mom kept looking at us all as if she was never going to see us again. I was afraid to look at her for fear I'd start crying or yell at her. No one else seemed to notice anything wrong so maybe it was all in my head, but I doubt it. And today I am sure that something is wrong. Dad was home, he has the whole weekend off, and he wanted to go out with Mom but she refused. She said, "It's your day off, not mine, I have a lot of things to do. All my life I've accommodated myself to your vacations, to your time off—I'm supposed to drop everything when you say the word. Well, I'm sorry, but I'm not doing it anymore. This is a big city, and I'm sure you can find something to amuse yourself."

Dad was in a rage. "I guess I had the notion that you enjoyed a vacation with me—that you might like to spend a day with me. You're just getting a lot of cock-eyed ideas in your head from those damned women's groups you go to."

Then Mom did something that really scared me. She picked up his untouched copy of *The New York Times,* crumpled it all up, and threw it at him. He looked so surprised. Then he laughed, which I suppose was the worst thing he could have done. "You didn't have to ruin my *Times,*" he said. "There are a lot better things to throw than a newspaper."

Mom grabbed her coat and ran out of the house.

The whole day was awful. Didi went off with Eric, and I hung around because I didn't want to leave Dad alone. But staying home didn't seem to do much good: Dad wandered around looking depressed and terrible, picking up books and putting them down, drinking coffee and smoking, which he had given up. After a lousy lunch he asked me if I wanted to go for a walk, and I said okay, but it was cold and windy so we didn't walk far. Then he sat in the living room and I sat in my room waiting to see if Mom was coming home. Every time I heard the elevator stop at our floor my heart jumped—I wanted her to come home but I was scared of what would happen when she did.

But nothing happened. She came home and fixed supper. She asked me what I did all day and I told her "Nothing."

"That's silly when you have a holiday," she said. She didn't ask Dad anything, and I think she was annoyed that I stayed home with him.

I hate what's going on—it all seems so stupid. It isn't as if either one of them was doing anything bad, like getting drunk or having love affairs. We used to be a real family. I wonder if they wish they hadn't ever gotten married and had kids. . . .

Saturday after Thanksgiving

It's happened. They had a big fight about me. I wish I'd never been born.

It started so simply. I said I was going to spend the day with Roger. Big deal. So Dad asked me who Roger was, and I told him a boy in my class.

"But who is he? That doesn't tell me anything," says he.

"What do you want to know about him? He's tall and good looking, he's got curly hair and he's very smart in math."

"Has your mother met him? Does she know anything about his parents?"

"No, Mom hasn't met him. How could she

meet him, he's never been here, and she's never home anyway. For God's sake, I'm not marrying him. I'm just going out with him today."

Then Mom appeared. "What's this cross-examination all about?"

Then Dad let loose. Did she know she still had a young daughter in the house, and why the hell wasn't she home taking care of me instead of running around with a lot of nonsense . . . he was sick and tired of what was going on, and she never should have had children if she wasn't prepared to take care of them until they were grown up . . . blah, blah, blah . . .

So Mom screamed at him that a father had responsibilities too, but all he wanted to do was to give orders and do nothing. If he cared about who his kid's friends were why didn't he find out himself instead of being a stupid jackass and asking a lot of dumb questions and screaming at her, and blah, blah, blah . . .

I yelled at both of them to shut up and leave me alone. "I'm old enough to take care of myself and pick my own friends." I went into my room and slammed the door.

I know that they both wish I wasn't around. Didi doesn't count anymore because she's "grown up" (yeah, yeah). Anyway, they leave her alone. I used to feel sorry for Millie because her mother went off to make movies and she had to stay with neighbors, and her father wasn't around at all, but that was different. Her mother had to make money. This is worse. We live together as if we were a happy family but we're not.

December

I went to Kathy's house for the first time today. It's fantastic. She has two sisters, one older and one younger, and they seem to honestly like each other. They have a brother too, but I didn't meet him. But they talk about him as if he were some- one fabulous. Toni (short for Antoinette) is the younger one, and Penelope (who refuses to be called Penny) is sixteen, and she sat and talked with us as if we were her own age—she didn't even treat Toni, who's only eleven, like a baby. Adam (the brother) is between Kathy and Penelope, so I guess he's around fifteen.

They live in this terrific renovated brownstone on Ninetieth Street, and they have two top floors to themselves. Kathy has a room with Toni, and Penelope and Adam have their own rooms and on the top floor there's a big playroom filled with all their stuff. All their rooms are fixed up differently. I liked Kathy's the best. She has two Siamese cats and she has pictures of cats all over the room, and a big old fur rug, and millions of plants, and old furniture. I felt a little sad seeing the cats; they reminded me of my cat, Midnight. I miss her and keep wondering if she's still alive. She disappeared on Cape Cod last summer—she went out and never came back. We searched all over for her and even put up signs in the village, but we never found her. I cried for days. I hope that she found a good home.

Kathy's mother scared me at first. She's very tall and overpowering. She was wearing a long, flowing robe and a lot of beads. She reminded me of a spooky fortune teller I once saw in a country circus, except Kathy's mother has long, blond braids wound around her head. But she was very nice. She told us to go down to the kitchen (in the basement) and take what we wanted, so we made hot cocoa and whipped cream and ate a chocolate cake that was there. Kathy and her sisters weren't at all worried that their mother might be saving the cake for a dessert. I remembered Kathy saying she'd been fat, but no one mentioned it until Toni said, "I'm glad Kathy can eat everything now." She explained that she'd had to take medicine for her glands and had been on a strict diet. The way they did things together and talked to each other was what made them so terrific.

They told me about a trip they'd all made to Mexico last summer. They traveled in a van their father had fixed up, and camped out in sleeping bags.

Toni said, "I did a lot of the cooking." Instead of putting her down because she was the youngest, Kathy and Penelope said what a fantastic cook she was and they wished she'd make pancakes for them next Sunday. They all said such *good* things about each other, especially about Adam. "He spoke the best Spanish," Kathy said, and Penelope said he'd caught the most fish. Then Penelope changed the subject.

"Kathy said you want to be a writer."

"I think I do," I told her.

"She writes terrific stories," Kathy said.

"Maybe you'll write a movie someday," Toni suggested. "And we'll produce it," said Kathy and Penelope.

"Yeah, yeah," I laughed.

"No fooling," Toni said.

"We made . . ." Kathy started.

"Two short ones," Penelope interrupted.

"Pretty bad," Kathy commented.

"They were good, I liked them," Toni said.

"Someday . . ." Kathy looked at Penelope and they both laughed.

"Someday for real," Penelope said.

I had the feeling that they were serious and that they would do it. I had never met a family like them—they were smart and serious, but not in a snobby way, and their seriousness wasn't dull and bookish—they could be silly and funny. But they were serious about themselves in a way that made me feel that I wanted them to take me on as a friend. Being their friend would make me feel good about myself—something Grandma often talked about. "You are a valuable person," she's said to me, "and you have to hold that value in esteem, not waste yourself and your talents carelessly. Wasting money is not nearly as serious as wasting yourself."

When I was leaving, Mrs. Stickney asked me to be sure to come back soon, and she said it as if she meant it, not just being polite.

I walked home thinking that something important had happened to me that afternoon, something I didn't know about yet or fully understand.

Still December

Actually this school isn't so bad. At least Mr. Bruce Travers, my English teacher, is pretty good, and that's the most important. I never had a man teacher I liked before (the only man I ever had was that creep Mr. Harris). Mr. T. is kind of old, he's got a white mustache and a brownish small beard, but he says funny things and sometimes very nice ones. Roger told me to keep the copy of Keats's poems, and he wrote in it "To Sarah, who might have inspired 'La Belle Dame Sans Merci.'" That made me feel sophisticated which I'm not, but I guess he thinks I'm "without mercy," because I haven't let him kiss me. Yet. Holding hands with him makes me uncomfortable and God only knows what a kiss would do. I want to kiss him but I'm scared. Anyway Mr. T. picked up my book and saw the inscription. He didn't laugh, he only said, "I would have let it go with 'La Belle Dame.'" And now he sometimes says, "And how is La Belle Dame today?" No one's ever called me a beautiful lady before.

Sometimes I wish that Roger wasn't in my classes—that he went to a different school. He makes me nervous. It isn't his fault, it's just that when I feel he's looking at me, I get self-conscious.

Almost Christmas

I hate where I'm at. I can't even get excited about Christmas. I think that's awful, being only thirteen years old and not caring about Christmas. I never expected everything to be so different so soon. Maybe I'm queer not aching to be grown up. Millie says she can't wait to be eighteen so that she can do whatever she wants, but I can't think of anything I want to do. Growing up can be an awful headache.

Last night, Didi came into my room.

"Listen," she said, "has Mom said anything to you?"

"About what?"

"I think she's up to something. I just wondered if she talked to you."

"I thought you were the one she confided in. I'm just the kid around here."

"Come off it. Stop feeling sorry for yourself." She was looking at herself in the mirror while she was talking. But then she turned around. "I don't want to be here for Christmas and I'm afraid there's going to be a blowup."

"I imagine there would be." This was the last straw. For Didi not to even care about Christmas, not needing to be home—it was too much. I felt as if I didn't have any family at all, and when I thought of the Stickneys I wanted to cry. "Where are you planning to go?" I asked.

"Eric and I want to go skiing."

"Can't you go after Christmas? Even the day after?"

"No, we want to spend Christmas together." She gave me an almost human look. "You shouldn't count on me anymore, Sarah. I'm going to be getting out of here soon and you're going to have to keep the home fires burning."

"Maybe we'll all burn up," I said glumly. "Where are you going?"

"I'm not going back to school next semester. I'm going to live in Boston."

"With Eric?"

She stared at me for a few seconds. "Yes, with Eric. But for God's sake, keep your mouth shut."

"Aren't you going to tell Mom and Dad?"

"I will when I'm ready. But if you breathe a word, I'll kill you."

"With a gun, or your bare hands?" I asked.

"Don't be an idiot. Aren't you shocked?" She asked the question as if she wanted me to be.

"Of course not. Nothing you do would shock me."

"You really are a brat!" she shouted.

I gave that a few minutes' thought. I suppose, when it comes to her, she's right. Somehow nasty things just pop out even though I don't always mean them.

Christmas Eve afternoon

I hope I don't drown this page with tears, all hell just broke loose. Stupid Didi waited until this morning to announce that she was leaving to go skiing with Eric. So of course Dad promptly said that she couldn't go. I'm sure Mom would have said the same thing if he hadn't said it first. But his words took the lid off a hot kettle that had been boiling inside Mom. She really let go!

"And why shouldn't she go?" demanded Mom. "She's old enough to know what she wants to do. I suppose you think she shouldn't go away with a boy. Don't you trust your own daughter to know how to behave?"

"I don't think she's old enough to go away with

a boy and furthermore I like to have my daughters home for Christmas," said Dad.

Well, Dad let himself in for it. "Oh, yes, what *you* like is the most important thing in the world. You've been living in a fool's paradise, but you had better forget it now. That's past history. We are not arranging our lives around you anymore —we are going to please ourselves."

"Why don't you speak for yourself? If your daughters want to be independent I think they can speak for themselves, instead of being brainwashed by you."

That really got Mom mad. She yelled at him and said things much worse than male chauvinist pig.

Then Didi got into it. She said she wasn't interested in listening to them go at each other like a couple of fishwives, and that they may as well know now that she was not going back to school, but was going up to Boston after the end of the semester to live with Eric.

Mom gulped at that, but she was trapped. I think she would have liked to back down, but she couldn't. It was insane to listen to their ridiculous fight when I knew that deep down they agreed, that neither one of them wanted Didi to go off to Boston to live with Eric. But by this time they weren't even listening to each other, just screaming away, until finally Mom left the room in tears.

And Didi took off, and here we are, on Christmas Eve—Mom sulking in her room, Dad out for a walk, and me wishing I could do something but not knowing what. At least Grandma's coming over tonight. Maybe that will help.

Day after Christmas

I wish Didi was home. This is probably the first time in my life I honestly need her. I think Mom is leaving home and I don't know what to do. I don't know if I should call Grandma—although I have an awful feeling no one can do any good now.

Christmas Eve was pretty grim, but not nearly so bad as Christmas Day, because at least Grandma was here Christmas Eve. They told her about Didi, and she was pretty upset but she at least had some humor about it. At one point when Mom and Dad started arguing she actually burst out laughing. "You two sound like a skit on women's lib," she said. "You've lost Didi, and you're both on soapboxes. Let's talk about Didi, and what kind of boy Eric is. There's nothing new about two people living together, it's been going on for a long time. The point is whether it's good for Didi and, if not, whether either one of you can do anything about it. Which, by the way, I rather doubt."

"Eric's a drip," I said. But Grandma bawled me out because I had to confess that I hardly knew him, and she said, among other things, that I wasn't being very helpful. It turned out that nobody really knew Eric, and that got Grandma pretty mad. It also got Dad going after Mom again, saying it was her business to know who her kids were going out with, that she was the one who was home, blah, blah, blah. And of course Mom said it was just as much his responsibility as hers, except that she trusted her daughters and treated them like mature human beings, blah, blah, blah. So Grandma had to shut them both up again. Finally Mom played some Christmas carols, but no one's heart was in it.

Later I went over to Kathy's house, but I couldn't stand it. They were all so damned happy. I once read someplace that people who were content may as well be cows chewing their cud in a field, but I think that's crazy. The Stickneys aren't like cows at all. They have fun, and Mrs. Stickney doesn't seem the least bit unhappy because she markets and cooks and makes clothes for the girls. She seems to *enjoy* it. But then she doesn't mind if the house gets into an awful mess, and it does; if she feels like dropping everything and going off to do something else, she goes. I think that's a good way to be. The trouble with Mom is that she wants everything in the house just so—if everything isn't vacuumed once a week you'd think the world was coming to an end—but she hates to do it.

Still Christmas vacation

I can't decide if I really like Roger or not, even though he knows an awful lot. When you walk around the Village with him, he knows where to get the best pizza and which shop has the best leather things, and where there are bargain Indian blouses, and when you go into a junk store or a secondhand bookstore he has a nose for finding the choice bargains. I do get worried about why he likes me. I keep thinking there must be some ulterior motive—I mean I'm not bad looking but I'm not that pretty, and I'm not sophisticated the way Millie is.

He took me to the movies last night and when we came home no one was there. He sat down at

Mom's piano and started playing old songs from the forties and fifties—I couldn't believe that he knew all the lyrics. He made me sit down next to him on the bench, and I felt kind of silly sitting there listening to him sing. As if we were putting on an act, except that I had nothing to do.

Then suddenly he turned around and started kissing me. I guess he thought the music would put me in the mood, but it didn't. I was too nervous being alone in the house with him.

"Don't you like me?" Roger asked.

"Of course I like you. I wouldn't see you if I didn't."

"Don't you want to kiss me?"

"Well, yes, I do. But not here."

That made Roger laugh. "This is better than the park, isn't it? Much warmer."

"Maybe it's too warm," I giggled foolishly.

"I'm crazy about you, Sarah," Roger said.

"I hear the elevator. I think my parents are coming."

We both listened, but it was the people in the next apartment.

"Did anyone ever tell you that you have a nice body?" Roger asked.

I didn't know what to say.

Then he grabbed me and started to kiss me again.

"Hey, what are you doing?" I hollered.

"I'm crazy about you," he said.

I was curious about what was going to happen next but I was scared so I pushed him away. I pushed him hard, and he rolled over on to the floor.

"I'm sorry . . . I really am . . ."

"It's all right," he said coldly. "I thought you liked me, but I guess I'm wrong."

"You're not wrong! I do like you, I really do. I'm just scared."

Roger laughed without really laughing.

He made me feel awful.

"I'm nervous about my parents coming home," I said, which was only half the truth. I didn't want this to be the end.

"Well, I'm going home," he said, and he left without kissing me goodbye.

I was very upset. I took a bath and looked at my body in the mirror. I would never have the nerve to let Roger see it. I suppose I will die an old maid.

January

If I had any hopes that the New Year was going to be better I sure was wrong.

I think Mom has gone bananas. She called Didi and me in for a talk. She was pale and twitchy, walking around the room, picking up clean ashtrays and putting them down. I don't remember all her exact words, but this was the jist of it:

"I'm going to be living downtown for a while," she said. "I hope I can make you girls understand that I need to do this. It's not that I don't love all of you, I do, very much, but I have to figure some things out for myself and this seems to be the only way I know how. I'm going to live with two women friends who have a loft in Soho—one's a painter and one is a sculptor. I intend to work on my piano—not just play, but compose. I need to be on my own, away from here."

Didi spoke first. "You mean you're leaving Dad? Are you getting divorced?"

"No! I'm not getting divorced," Mom snapped. "I'm not doing anything but giving myself some time, by myself."

"You mean with two other women," said Didi, unsympathetically.

"Have you told Dad?" I asked. I was stunned, even though I knew a disaster had been brewing.

"I intend to tell him today." She looked from one to the other of us, she was close to crying. "I thought you girls would understand—you're women too, you should know how hard it is . . ."

"How hard what is?" yelled Didi.

"To be a mother and a wife and still be yourself. I feel that I'm missing the boat. I was brought up with old-fashioned ideas about being a woman and now everything is changing. You girls won't have this trouble, you're lucky. I thought you'd understand . . ."

"You're too old to change," said Didi. "You should be satisfied with your own generation!"

Mom was horrified. "I'm only forty-six. That's not old! You kids think anyone over twenty is old. It's mean! You want all the changes for yourself. You want to be free but you don't want me to be. Well, I intend to have my *own* life!"

She looked good standing there with her eyes flashing at Didi, and I was proud of her. Proud and sad too, because she looked old and tired. She had dark rings under her eyes, and I had the feeling that she was off on some wild-goose chase. She spoke strong but she looked worried.

"Do you have to leave to find out what you want?" I asked. I couldn't conceive of her leaving.

"I'm afraid so, darling . . ." She knelt down and hugged me hard. "I shouldn't be doing this to you. You're too young and I don't want to hurt you."

"I'm not so young, I'll be okay," I lied.

"Well, I hope so," said Didi, "because I'm not going to be here. I'm going to live in Boston."

Mom stared at her. "Can't you wait a few months? So Sarah won't be alone with Dad?"

"No, I can't!" shouted Didi. "And I don't see why I should. Sarah's not my daughter, she's yours. If you're worried about her, then *you* stay home. Anyway, it's where you belong."

"Nobody's got to stay home with me," I shouted. "I can take care of myself!"

I couldn't wait for both of them to go away. I needed time to be alone, to think. I couldn't believe what was happening.

When I was alone in my room, I sat and tried to sort everything out. But I kept thinking about

Mom and I felt stuffed with sobs that wouldn't come out.

Later Mom stuck her head in my room and said that she was going out for a while and that she'd be back soon.

"When are you going to tell Dad?" I asked.

"Tonight," she said.

That evening

They're in the living room talking. Didi is out, of course. I have the awful feeling that once Mom leaves she'll never come back. It's as if she were dying. I'm glad she isn't but in a way this is almost worse, because she's alive and I won't be with her. Maybe she'll meet some kids she loves better. Maybe she'll meet a man she'll love more than Dad. I'm NEVER going to let her know how I feel. If she wants to leave, let her! I'll take care of myself and Dad too—we don't need her.

Next afternoon

This has been the worst day of my life.

When I came home from school Mom was gone. I didn't know it at first. I looked in the hall closet and her fur coat (Dad gave it to her last year for Christmas) was still there. Then I went to her closet and a lot of clothes were still there. I felt relieved. But then I went into my room and there was a note on my desk. She said how much she loved me, and to take care and she gave me her address. Said she'd call me tonight to give me her phone number. I didn't know what to do.

I thought about Millie a little because she has an odd mother and no father, but she says that she doesn't mind anymore. I can't imagine not minding. There are kids in school whose parents are divorced, but that's different. At least they know where they're at. I don't know anyone whose mother has taken off, saying that she loves us all. How can you love someone and not want to be with them? I wonder if I'll stop loving her because she's left me. Can you stop loving your own mother?

I was alone in the house and I went to Mom and Dad's room. Some of her things were still around—I guess she didn't take much, and maybe that means she'll be back soon. But even if she does come back, I'll never know how she really feels.

When Didi came home, she found a note too. She was furious and tore it into bits. "I think it's disgusting," she said. "She thinks she's a teenager—going off to live in a loft—it's ridiculous. The kids downtown will laugh at her."

She made me angry. "She has rights too," I shouted. "All you care about is what people will say!" I wanted to hit her. She made me defend Mom when I wasn't even sure I wanted to.

"It doesn't matter to me," she said. "I'm moving over the weekend. I don't care if I never see her again."

She was so obnoxious I couldn't talk to her. You'd think she'd have some feelings for me. I hate her.

I was nervous about Dad coming home. I

didn't know what to expect. Mom had left a dinner ready on the stove, which was pretty silly since we were going to have to cook for ourselves from now on anyway.

Later that night

Dad came home with a cheerful phony front. "Cheers," he said over his before-dinner drink. "I guess it's you and me together now. How do you like the idea of taking care of your old man?"

I drank my tomato juice glumly. If his cheerfulness was for me, I didn't need it.

"Don't look so gloomy." The cheeriness was cracking. He started pacing up and down the room. "For Christ's sake, Sarah, you're not at a funeral. So your mother decided she needs to be alone for a while. It's not the end of the world. What if she had to be in a hospital, which thank God she isn't? We'd manage, wouldn't we?"

"This is different."

"Where's Didi tonight?" he asked, changing the subject.

"Out."

"That's obvious. Is she still insistent on moving up to Boston?"

"You'll have to ask her."

"Come on, honey, snap out of it. I'm not happy either, but sitting around moping doesn't help much."

"Maybe it helps me. When I feel mopey, I'm mopey. I don't feel like putting on an act. Maybe if you expressed some feelings things would be different around here."

Dad looked startled. "Hey, wait a minute. You'd better explain that."

"You give orders but you don't show your *feelings*. Except moping behind your newspaper. It's like you want to push everything under the rug. You never say what you *feel*. You never say that you're sad or hurt!"

"So my younger daughter's a psychologist? Where do you get those ideas from, anyway?"

"See, that's what I mean. You're not even talking about what I said. You're going right past it, like what I said didn't mean anything, and it does mean something."

"Okay, okay. I need time to think. Besides, I'm hungry now, let's eat."

He's never going to change. He doesn't listen, ever. He wants to tell everyone what to do but he never listens. Maybe that's why Mom left, maybe she wants someone who listens.

January

This is the worst time of year. We had a little snow, not enough to have any fun, just enough to get dirty and make the streets a mess. Didi hasn't moved yet, but I think she's really going this weekend. I was hoping her boyfriend was going to ditch her, she was acting so glum, but no such luck.

Now I have dates with my mother. It's ridiculous. I still haven't seen her loft. I think she's ashamed of it—she said it wasn't all fixed up yet and she'd rather I wait to come down until it was. We met on Eighth Street on Saturday. I almost cried when I saw her. I didn't even recognize her walking down the street—she looked like one of those crazy ladies you see on the street, not like anyone's mother. She was wearing jeans, a crazy, raggedy coat with fringes, a floppy hat, and high-heeled boots. She didn't have on any makeup, and she looked a hundred years old. I thought, oh, God, if this is her *real* self, she's flipped. I think she thought she looked young and with it.

She was very gay. She took my arm and said, "This is such fun, having a date with my daughter. It makes me feel like a teen-ager again."

I wanted to say that being a teen-ager wasn't so great, but I didn't. We went into the shops and she bought herself and me each a pair of earrings. But she acted so giddy, laughing and trying to joke with the sales people, I was embarrassed. She flirted with a young man with a beard who was half her age. She insisted on buying us each a hot dog, which I really didn't want, but she seemed to think it was important.

I was never so depressed in my life as when I left her. It was like being with a stranger who was terribly familiar at the same time. I love her, but I wish she wasn't acting so silly. I asked her if she was going back to her shrink (she saw him for quite a while a couple of years ago), and she looked at me wide-eyed. "Of course not. I don't need a doctor anymore. I need my freedom —I used to be tied up in knots, but I'm not anymore." I wonder if she is free, whatever the hell that means.

When I left her I went to see Grandma. I thought I could talk to her about Mom, but I didn't know what to say. I couldn't say that I thought Mom was nuts. She talked to me a little. "This is a rough time for you, I know. I've thought about asking your father if I should move in with you, but I decided against it. If he wants me, he'll ask, but honestly I think it's better that I don't. We have to assume that whatever is going on is temporary, and I don't want to make any move that smacks of permanence."

"I can manage okay," I told her. "Mom's been out so much lately anyway that this isn't all that different."

"You're a gutsy kid," Grandma said.

That's my trouble, I thought, people thinking that I'm gutsy, but they should know how my gut goes in for nose dives.

"How are things at school?" Grandma asked.

"Boring."

"I thought you liked school. How's the writing going?"

I told her that it was pretty good. As a matter of fact, I've written a couple of stories that my teacher liked. But I'm not so sure about being a writer. I think maybe I'd like to be a psychiatrist or psychologist. I like to figure out people, or try to. When I told Mr. T. about liking to psych out people he said that a good writer, especially a novelist, did that naturally. "You have to understand people to write about them," he said, "know what makes them tick and their relationship to others." He's really cool. You can talk to him about anything, and he never treats you like a kid. He said he wanted to invite me to his house for tea one afternoon—that would be cool.

"If I could have English and social studies all day school would be okay," I told Grandma. "The rest is boring."

Grandma seemed preoccupied.

"Do you think Mom'll come home soon?" I asked her.

"I hope so." Her face was unhappy. "She doesn't talk to me much these days. I'm afraid she thinks I disapprove of what she's doing, and maybe I do. But I do try to see things from her point of view, and to understand that she does what she has to do. I'm worried about Didi. For Didi this is the worst time for your mother to be away."

"No one's going to stop Didi. I think she's leaving this weekend."

I had the feeling that there were a lot of things Grandma wanted to talk to me about, but she never did. There was a wall between us that had never been there before. As if she knew things that I should know but that she didn't want to tell me. I don't like it even though I know some of it's my fault because I'm keeping things back. Oh, God, I hope I never lose Grandma for my friend.

February

As if I didn't have enough troubles, Millie had
to hand me more. She told me a story about
Roger. I don't know whether or not to believe
her. I hate not believing someone I know, but so
many people tell lies. I do myself, sometimes, but
not about anything important, or to someone I
trust. I've been thinking a lot about trusting
people lately. I always thought I could trust Mom
and Dad completely, and Grandma, of course,
but now I'm not so sure. I keep feeling that a
lot is going on that they're not telling me. They
expect me to be grown up and to take everything
in my stride, but they're not leveling with me.
They count on me to behave in a grown-up way,

but they keep things from me. It's not fair and it gets me mad.

Back to Millie. She said that Roger went to her house when no one was home (no one's ever home at Millie's—which she knew perfectly well before she let Roger go home with her). Anyway, she said that he made her take her blouse off.

"How can he make you?" I asked her.

"He pulled it off," she told me. When I asked her what he did after that, she wouldn't tell me. All she said was that taking off her blouse was only part of it, and that I knew perfectly well what he did. Of course I didn't know, but I didn't tell her that. I know how babies are made, but I didn't think Millie and Roger would be that stupid—and besides, she'd have to take off more than her blouse for that. Millie said that Roger was a terrible boy and that I'd better be careful going out with him.

He hasn't ever wanted to do anything except kiss me, and that's not so bad. I think Millie had to have something to do with it. If she really hadn't wanted to take off her blouse I think she could have stopped him. I'm sure I could. I think a girl can stop a boy if she wants to, and it's up to her to decide. It isn't as if Roger's a sex maniac—he's a kid in our class.

I think Millie told me that so I would stop seeing Roger. But she's wrong—she's not scaring me off. The trouble is, I'm not so sure about Roger myself. When I'm with him I like him, but then, when he's not there and I think about him, I get nervous because I don't feel absolutely comfortable with him—he makes me feel sexy. I feel as if he has some power that is stronger than mine, and I don't like that.

February

Two important things happened. One, Didi left for Boston. She wouldn't even go down to see Mom before she left, and Dad was furious—not about that so much as her going. He yelled at her and then sulked, but it was different. He kept muttering that her mother should be home, and that he couldn't be expected to handle two teen-age girls alone and that women's lib was wrecking families . . . he seemed helpless and sad, as if life was too much for him. I felt sorry for him because I wished we had a family too.

And Didi was pretty mean. She said, "There's nothing so great about staying in this house. You can't criticize me, with you and Mom behaving like a couple of ten-year-olds. It's ridiculous. I'm going and that's that. You can't stop me."

Dad shut up but you could tell he was miserable. After she left I asked if he wanted to go to the movies but he said no. I didn't know what to do. It's awful to see your own father look as if he wants to cry. We sat in the living room pretending to look at a stupid TV show. Then Dad got out a bottle of bourbon and proceeded to drink it straight. I'd never seen him drunk and I didn't know what to expect. He didn't do anything for a while, just sat there downing the stuff, looking gloomy. Then he banged down his glass and said, "Goddamn, goddamn, goddamn." Then he started crying! "I'm a goddamned failure. I've failed every which way. I failed as a husband, now I'm failing as a father, I failed as a painter . . . I'm fifty years old and nothing has gone right. I'll probably lose my job, I haven't even made it as a designer. Look at me, Sarah. How does it feel to have a failure for a father?"

"How should I know?" I said. "My father isn't a failure." I knew he wouldn't have talked that way if he hadn't drunk so much, but I think he meant it too.

81

His face was all screwed up so you could hardly see his eyes, but I thought I saw a smile flicker through. "That's what you think, but you're wrong. You may as well face it, you're stuck with a father who's no damned good."

"Don't tell me what I'm stuck with," I said. I couldn't bear to see him this way, and it made me angry, too. "I don't even know what you're talking about when you say you're a failure. I don't know what you expected to be."

"I was going to be a great painter," he said. "I was going to lead the simple life, never do a commercial line——I was going to only paint and paint, not care about money, not care about possessions . . . and look at me. I haven't touched a canvas in years, I'm in debt, my wife has left me, Didi treats me like a half-wit, I doubt you have much use for me . . ."

"Why don't you paint now?" I asked.

I didn't think he heard me because he didn't answer. Then he said, "It's too late. I'm too old. I've established a way of life I can't get out of. I'm trapped."

His words sounded familiar. Just like Mom's. I don't understand about traps. Why can't grown-ups get out of them? If I were trapped I'd just get out.

"This is a free country. Why can't you get out? It's not like you were in prison or a labor camp. You can do what you want to do. Who's stopping you from painting?"

Dad looked at me like I was saying something strange. "It's a free country only if you have a lot of money. I've got three people dependent on me, I've got to earn money."

He got me mad. "Nuts. Lots of people paint who aren't rich. We don't need a lot of money. We could live in our house in Truro and you could paint if you wanted to."

"We'd still have to eat, honey. At my age and with my responsibilities you don't just throw over a job for nothing. I might never sell a painting for years, if then. I'd have to be crazy."

"We could all get jobs. Mom, Didi, and me. I could work after school."

"You're a dear, sweet child, but you don't know what you're talking about. What the three of you could earn wouldn't even pay our taxes."

"Don't call me a sweet child," I yelled. "Maybe you don't know what you're talking about. You're scared, that's what."

I hit home and I was sorry. He looked miserable. "Yes, I'm scared. I don't even know if I can paint. I used to think so, but that was a long time ago. I told you, I'm a failure, and you may as well know it now as ever."

God, he got me so angry I wanted to shake him. "You're not a failure," I shouted. "You've done a lot, and if you really want to be a painter, you still can. You're just feeling sorry for yourself. When I grow up I'm going to do what I want to do, and nothing's going to stop me."

"I hope you will," he said, but I don't think he really believed it.

But I do. I believe that people can do what they want to do. I can't see why not. Nobody needs to have a lot of clothes and furniture and stuff like that, and if you want to do something you do it, no matter what anyone says. I wish I could convince Dad, but he thinks I don't know anything. Maybe I don't know all the things he knows, but he didn't tell me anything to prove that he is right.

The other thing that happened is that I met Kathy's brother Adam. He probably wouldn't know me if he fell over me but he's the most remarkable person I've ever met. He's like no one else. He's not good looking the way Roger is, he has a long, bony face, with big, strong features (nose and chin), his hair's not very long, rather short in fact and in curls. He has very blue eyes, and when he looks at you, you know he's really seeing you. (Maybe he would remember me—I have to take back that he wouldn't.) He came in when Kathy and her sisters and I were just sitting around having a Coke, and he calmly announced he'd just written a poem. And he read it to us, just like that, without being shy or making a fuss. And he cared about what we thought—his *sisters*, and a kid sister's friend. I thought it was a beautiful poem. The others discussed it more critically, and he didn't mind a bit. He listened and said yes and no, and then said he was going to work on it some more. I've never seen a family like that—they *listen* to each other. I'll never in my life know a boy like Adam. He'd have to have a girl who was beautiful and smart and very special. I mustn't even think about him —it would be like thinking about the Prince of Wales (who looks kind of dopey in his pictures), but Adam is that far away. I guess I'll always be stuck with the Rogers of the world.

Sometimes I wonder if I like Kathy because of her family. To be perfectly honest, I think it has something to do with it, but Grandma says there's nothing wrong with that, as long as that's not the only reason. Kathy is easygoing and fun and that has to have something to do with her

family, I think. And it's fun to go to her house—
and part of that is because they make a big fuss
about me. I don't care what anyone says, it is
nice to be admired and made to feel important.

March

It finally happened. I went down to my mother's apartment. She invited me for lunch. It is certainly peculiar to be invited by your own mother for lunch. I said apartment, but it's not really an apartment. It's a big loft, and I couldn't believe my mother was living there. She used to be so fussy about her furniture and rugs and all her dishes and silver and stuff, and now she's living on bare floors, with an old, raggedy sofa, pillows instead of chairs, and very little privacy. The two other women seem to belong there, but she looked out of place. And not very happy. She said she was heartbroken about Didi because she hadn't heard from her. "I've called her so many times, but she's never there, or at least that dreadful boy says she's not. I don't always believe him. I've written to her but she doesn't answer. I'm afraid she doesn't approve of me."

"What do you care? You're doing what you want to do—and you said that's what counts."

Mom gave me a strange look. "Yes, of course. Tell me about you. And about Dad? How are you getting along?"

"We're okay."

"How are things at school?"

"All right, I guess. Boring as ever."

"How's your writing coming along?"

"Pretty good." I had written a story that Mr. T. said was remarkable, but I couldn't get myself to tell her about it. I honestly didn't know how to talk to her. She didn't seem like my mother but like another person. I felt so sad sitting with her because she didn't know how to talk to me, either. After lunch she suggested that we go out, and we walked around looking at some of the galleries. The pictures looked pretty awful to me—I liked the paintings up at the Metropolitan Museum better, the ones Millie used to take me to see. The pictures my mother said she liked (I couldn't believe she really liked them) were blotches of color that didn't mean a darn thing, or were of crazy looking people.

Mom asked me if I was in love with Roger, and I said that was the craziest thing I ever heard. I told her I was only thirteen years old (which naturally she knew, unless she'd forgotten—anything seemed possible) and that I didn't even know what it felt like to be in love. Then she went all gaga and said that to love was the most beautiful experience in the world, that it was what counted most of anything, and that she was glad that she loved so many people, Dad and Didi and me, and Maude and Patricia (the two women she was living with), and that sometimes she loved people she hardly knew like the old lady in the stationery store, and an old man she saw picking at the garbage pails every morning. She said that she loved the human race.

"Do you love murderers, like the men who killed the Kennedys, or the man who killed the woman a few blocks from our house last week?" I asked her.

"I have compassion for them," she said. "They are sick people because we have a sick society. We are living in evil times, but there are some of us who are trying to get back to what is honest and healthy and real."

I didn't see anything so honest and real about leaving a pretty decent apartment for what she had now, and Dad and Didi and me if she loved us so much, although I had to leave Didi out of it because she wasn't home anyway.

When I was leaving she asked me to give Dad her love, and again she told me what a wonderful person he was and how sorry she was if she was hurting him now.

I didn't bother to ask her why she was doing it, because I knew if she had a good reason (which I doubted) I'd never hear it.

Riding home on the subway was scary. A bunch of boys kept staring at me, and I was afraid they were going to grab me or my pocketbook. After 59th Street there was no one else in the car but them and me, and I was afraid to get up to walk into another car because I didn't want them to know I was afraid—so I sat there pretending to read the ads but quaking inside.

I felt myself getting really mad at Mom. If she hadn't left us to live way downtown I wouldn't have to take that awful subway ride.

March

This was a beautiful day. It started off right when I got my math paper back. I got a B+. Miracle of miracles. Roger got an A (of course) and so did Kathy, but I was pleased with my B+. I'll tell Dad as soon as he comes home.

Kathy and I went to the park after school. It was a gorgeous day, almost like spring, and we walked and talked a lot. She told me that Adam thought I was very interesting looking—that really set me up, although I told her I wasn't sure what he meant. Kathy said, "It means you have personality and style—you don't look like everyone else."

"Yeah, that I'm a freak."

"Sure, you have four eyes and two noses. No, Adam liked you. I think if you look interesting a person wants to get to know you better."

Naturally I couldn't tell Kathy how excited that made me, and, besides, I decided it was just something Adam would say and that it didn't mean anything. But it did make me feel good.

We walked around the zoo and bought peanuts and ice cream. I finally told Kathy about my mother. I hadn't meant to, but Kathy was terrific. "Sometimes I wish my mother would go away," she said.

"But your mother's fantastic. Your whole family is. You all get along so well," I said.

"We get along pretty well. But my mother can be a pain sometimes. She gets ideas, like we should stop eating meat or that it's healthy to live in a freezing house or all of a sudden she doesn't want us to watch television. She goes off on these kicks for a few weeks and we all sigh with relief when it's over, but then she's off on a new one. Even my father, who thinks it's amusing, sometimes gets annoyed. Once he got mad as hell when she tried to fix him lettuce sandwiches to take to his office for lunch. He thought she'd gone bananas."

I wanted to hear more about her family, but I didn't want to pry. I did get some comfort out of knowing that everything wasn't absolutely fantastic with them all the time. That's my mean streak, no doubt. We both agreed that mothers are much harder to get along with than fathers. "That's probably good," Kathy said, "because when we grow up we're going to have to live with a man, not a woman."

"I may never live with anybody," I told her. "No man may want me."

"That's ridiculous," Kathy said. "Millions of men will. But maybe you'll want to live alone."

"I don't think so. It would be too lonesome."

Later that night

It *was* a beautiful day, but the trouble is, something good doesn't last. Dad wasn't the least bit interested in my math paper. He glanced at it and said, "That's great," but his mind was far away. He spent the evening doing a lot of figuring, I think he's worried about money. He's got to be paying for Mom's loft because she hasn't any money. I'm going to make my own money when I grow up—it doesn't seem fair for Mom to do what she wants but for Dad to have to pay for it. She said that she was going to earn money, but she hasn't said anything about giving piano lessons.

March

My grandmother came over and cooked a fantastic supper for us. God, it was good to have a super meal for a change. I love to eat, and I'm glad I don't get fat. Even though I can't talk to her about some things now, I can still talk with her about a lot of other things. She told Dad that she didn't think Mom was happy. "I have a feeling she'd like to come home, but she doesn't know how without losing face."

"What difference would that make?" I asked. "If she wants to come home, why doesn't she just do it?"

Grandma gave Dad a funny look. "Maybe she'd like to be asked."

Dad shook his head. "No way. She has to do it on her own. She knows how I feel about it. She knows I think it's ridiculous for her to be living in that place."

Grandma sighed, but she gave me the eye (warning me to keep my mouth shut). But when we were alone (Dad went out to get cigarettes), I exploded. "He's just being stubborn. I can't believe those two. If she wants to come home, and he wants her to, how can they not do it?"

"Because everything isn't that simple," Grandma said. "People are complicated. I've told you that before. You see everything black and white, but there are a lot of grays, especially in relationships. It isn't just love and hate. People have pride and fears. Maybe he's afraid of being rejected if he asks her. Don't forget your father was very hurt by her leaving. As people get older they seem to develop more defenses, they're more afraid of sticking their necks out and getting hurt."

It still seemed simple to me, but Grandma said that's because I just see my parents as parents. "You just see one dimension, mother and father," she said—and I suppose she's right. It's hard to think of them as people with fears. A kid has fears but you never think of grown-ups having them.

Didi called up from Cambridge. I thought at first she just called to say hello, but before she finished she asked me to send her some special soap that she likes from Bloomingdale's. Of course I said I would, but at least I didn't say I'd rush right down to get it, but that I would when I was in the neighborhood. I'm getting smarter with Didi.

Still March

I don't know what to do. I mentioned to Kathy that I had to go downtown to see my mother (she wanted to have a date with me), and she said why didn't she go with me? That put me in a tizzy. I liked the idea of not going there alone, but I had qualms about Kathy meeting my mother and seeing her in that crummy loft. I feel like the worst rat in the world, but I was ashamed of my mother. I didn't want anyone to know what was going on in our family (although Kathy already knew about my mother), but seeing her was real, different from talking about her. I didn't know what to do. I know I shouldn't be ashamed but that's how I felt.

After school Kathy was waiting for me. When we arrived we coud hear my mother playing the piano inside. Kathy stopped to listen. "It's beautiful, isn't it? Is that your mother playing?"

I told her yes. The music did sound nice, and I had my fingers crossed that Mom wasn't going to be in one of her silly moods. She was wearing jeans and a shirt but she looked okay. I introduced her to Kathy.

"What were you playing?" Kathy asked.

"Just something I made up. I haven't put it down on paper yet."

Mom flushed when Kathy told her that the music was lovely. Kathy talked to my mother about music and she was terrific. Mom was so pleased, she adored Kathy, and the afternoon was fantastic. It was the first time I felt happy for weeks and weeks. I felt awful that I had been ashamed of Mom—Kathy thought she was marvelous. "She doesn't act like a mother," Kathy said. "She's a fantastic woman . . ."

It made me stop to think—Kathy admired Mom for exactly the things that drove me up the wall. Maybe kids never see their parents the way other people do. That makes me wonder what people think of me. Sometimes I wish I were a fly so I could fly around and listen in when the kids at school talk about me. What do they say? Probably that Sarah Grinnell's a creep. I don't really believe that, but I do wish I knew if they're saying I'm smart or dumb or attractive or ugly.

I was dying to get Kathy to talk about her brother, but I didn't know how. I did ask if he'd written any more poems, and she only laughed and said, "He's always writing poetry." But that was all.

Still March

I used to worry about Millie, and then I stopped, but now I'm bothered again. Cats are much easier than people—they don't get married and divorced and they have babies without any trouble. But I suppose people are more interesting.

Millie is so odd, sometimes she acts as if she's my best friend, and other times she is so standoffish. She asks me a million questions about Kathy, and I think she gets annoyed when I go out with Kathy. I can't imagine anyone being jealous of me. I hate talking about Kathy with Millie. She asks me what her family is like, and her house, and when I told her I thought they were all fantastic, she said that I get crushes on people too easily. She thinks I have a crush on Roger, which is not true. I really like most people but Millie puts them down. I like people and I want them to like me.

March

I knew there was something wrong with Millie. She told me that she missed her period and she thought she was pregnant. I was so shocked I didn't know what to say. She was very mysterious about who the boy was (I didn't ask her), except that he was much older and terrific. She acted very excited about it in a funny way, almost as if she was glad it had happened. I'd die if anything like that ever happened to me, but then it couldn't because I'd never let any boy get that close to me. When I asked Millie what she was going to do she said she hadn't decided, and she went into a long thing about wanting to have the baby—she sounded nuts—I couldn't imagine my friend Millie with a baby. She said there were marvelous homes where she could go and have it, and that she didn't care what her mother would say. She said that finally she would have someone who loved her and whom she loved too. She made me feel sad.

Still March

It's late at night—or, rather, early in the morning, about two A.M. Millie's asleep in Didi's room. She came over after supper, and it was an awful evening. She told me everything. She said that she made up the whole story about being pregnant, and the mysterious older man. She had missed her period, but the rest was a lie because she hadn't done anything with any boy. I was relieved when she said that, because it made her seem much closer to me and not like someone who'd stepped into another world. But then she cried and cried.

"I feel so alone," she sobbed. "I don't know why I do things like that. . . . I get all these crazy ideas and it's because no one loves me. I haven't anyone in the whole world who really cares about me, and so I thought if I had a baby I'd have someone, and I imagined a father—a beautiful man who would love me and my baby . . . we'd be a family. I hate being nobody, belonging to no one . . ."

"But you have your mother. She has to leave sometimes to go to work, but she comes home, and she loves you . . ."

"My mother wants to get rid of me. I heard her talking to her boyfriend. He wants her to go to Mexico to live. She said she would in a minute if it weren't for me. She wishes she never had me . . . she hates me for being alive. I told her to go, I'd take care of myself, but I'd die if she left me alone. I'm scared to even be in the house alone at night when she goes out."

"She's not going to go," I told Millie. "People say things they don't mean. I haven't told you, but my mother's gone away, she left home."

Millie was so surprised she stopped crying. "Your mother . . . I can't believe it. She's such a mouse."

"She's not a mouse. She's living in a loft with two other women. Listen, I think mothers don't want kids anymore, and we've got to do something about it."

"What can we do?"

"I don't know, but mothers are sick of staying home and taking care of houses and kids."

"They shouldn't have us if they don't want us," Millie said.

"It's too late now. We're here. Maybe we have to learn to get along without them. My mother says there's a woman's revolution going on. I think there has to be a kid's revolution . . . I mean we get them home or get along without them."

"I don't want to be left alone," Millie wailed. "I'm too scared."

"What are you scared of? You're alone a lot anyway. I don't think your mother's going to go away and leave you, but you've got to be prepared."

"How do I do that?"

"I guess by taking care of yourself. We've got to show them that we can be okay by ourselves."

I was talking big and I wished I felt as strong as I sounded. It was too late for her to go home alone so she called her mother (who natch was home when she wasn't there) and she stayed over. I've been thinking about our problem a lot. It's true: if we show our mothers that we can take care of ourselves it won't make so much difference whether they stay home or not. If only I can really do it . . .

April

Miracle of miracles. Didi called up and thanked me for sending the soap and asked me to come up for the weekend. I couldn't believe her. She actually said that she'd like me to come. Can't wait.

Still April

Dad gave me a hard time about going up to see Didi. He said that he didn't think it was right for a thirteen-year-old girl to visit a sister who was living with a boy. The craziest thing I ever heard. As if my visiting them was going to corrupt me. What do I care if they're married or not? I know they're living together, and seeing them wasn't going to change anything. I said I was going whether he liked it or not and that I'd borrow the money for my fare from a friend.

Dad said he didn't want me to borrow money, so he gave it to me. I'm going to take the train.

April

My life is extraordinary. Nothing turns out the way I expect it. I wonder if that happens to other people? Something has happened to Didi, maybe it's love. She was really glad to see me, and we had a wonderful time. I don't blame her for wanting to live in Cambridge, it's beautiful. Harvard Square has terrific shops and loads of kids. The streets have lovely old houses, and Harvard and the Charles River are beautiful. We watched Harvard men practicing rowing, and everywhere you go there are kids who seem to be having a good time.

Didi and Eric have bikes and they borrowed one for me, and we went biking in a park and stretched out on the grass and ate hot dogs. Even Eric was less of a drip than I'd thought; he was actually very nice to me and wouldn't let me pay for anything. We went to a Greek restaurant for supper and ate moussaka and they drank wine and gave me sips. That was Saturday. Sunday they took me to a zoo where we saw all kinds of birds and fed them corn seed we bought.

I think Didi is pretty happy although now that I am home I realize that she hasn't changed that much—not underneath. She didn't seem to care very much about Mom or Dad, and she hasn't changed her mind about Mom one bit. Talking about Mom was the one time we almost got into an argument. I felt peculiar because in a way I was hypocritical. When I'm with Mom I don't think much of what she's doing—it seems pretty silly, and I don't understand what she's getting out of it because she doesn't seem happy. But when Didi started to put Mom down, I automatically defended her and said things that I wasn't sure I meant.

"Mom's too old to be acting like a kid," Didi said, repeating what she had said before. "I think Dad's stupid to let her get away with it."

"What's she getting away with? She's got a right to do what she wants to do. Dad doesn't own her."

"No, but he's supporting her, and what's he

getting out of it? She's deserted him, and you, too."

"She hasn't deserted us yet. And besides, money isn't everything."

"It's a lot. You can't do anything without money."

I had no answer for that, although it doesn't seem right. If money was everything, everyone who was rich would be happy and everyone poor would be unhappy, and I don't believe that's true.

May

I love this time of year. I can go out with just
a sweater, no heavy coat, and the park is pretty,
and it doesn't get dark until real late. I wish I
could live someplace where it was like this all the
time, but then there wouldn't be any snow, and
I'd miss that.

Kathy invited me to a party. She said it was no
special occasion, just a party to celebrate spring,
and she was asking a few kids over. I didn't ask
her if Adam was going to be there, but I hope
he will be. Kathy asked me if I wanted to bring
Roger, and I said I'd have to think about it.

May

I'm not very bright. I always took for granted that Roger was around my age, but I discovered that he's fifteen. No wonder he is so sophisticated. I think he purposely didn't tell me before. He had something the matter with him once and lost a year of school, and had to go back. I don't think I should see him anymore, but I don't know if I have the courage to stop. Going out with Roger is like eating peanuts—if they, or he, aren't around, you don't care, but once you start it's hard to stop. But I don't think I'll ask him to Kathy's party.

May

I've never been to a party like Kathy's before. She didn't just have some kids over. It was a real party-party, with grown-ups as well as kids. It was awful getting dressed alone, with neither Mom nor Didi there to advise me what to wear. I tried on practically everything I owned, and finally decided on a long cotton skirt and a sweater top. I walked over by myself because it was at six o'clock—a supper party. Dad said he was going to pick me up at eleven.

When I first got there I wanted to turn around and run home because there were so many people I didn't know, and it looked so elegant, but Kathy said that was crazy and that she would stick with me and that I'd have a good time. There was a long table loaded with food, and maids served it buffet style. Kathy and I took our food to a little table, and Adam came and sat with us. I was so nervous I could hardly eat, but the food was so good (shrimps, fried chicken, little meat balls, and hot rolls) that I managed to stuff myself.

Adam said that he hated big parties, and I told him that I'd never been to one like this before.

"You're lucky," he said. "My mother loves to give big parties. But we don't have to pay any attention, we can have a good time by ourselves."

That sounded good to me, and I noticed that I was the only one from school Kathy had invited. The other kids all belonged to the parents who were there. But it turned out that we didn't stay by ourselves, and the party got to be fun. We played charades, murder, and word games. Everyone played together, the grown-ups and the kids. Then someone played the piano and one of the boys played a guitar, and we sang songs. I was having a wonderful time when my father arrived at eleven to take me home. I didn't want to go. Mrs. Stickney invited Dad to come in for a while, but he only wanted to stay a few minutes. I hated to go home.

Adam was very nice to me all evening. But I think he was doing it for Kathy because she had to move around and be with some of the other girls there.

On the way home I asked Dad why he wouldn't stay. "I'm not in the mood for parties," he said. "Especially with a bunch of strangers, although they seem like nice people. I'm glad you had a good time."

I've been thinking about the party ever since. It was like going into another world, but coming home I felt like Cinderella—back to the old gloom.

May

Gloom is no word for the atmosphere now. Kathy's party is probably the last good time I'll ever have in my life. DAD LOST HIS JOB. I don't know what will become of us now. The studio had to let four people go, so it wasn't his fault—it's the economy, he said. A lot of help that is, it only makes matters worse because he doesn't think he can get another job.

"Maybe I can get a job after school and Saturdays," I said. "I could baby-sit or deliver groceries."

Dad almost bawled. "That's very nice of you, dear, but I don't think that's the answer."

"What is?"

"I wish I knew . . . I just don't know." He looked so sad and forlorn I wanted to cry. I wished Mom were home. Dad must have been reading my thoughts because he said, "I don't want you to run and tell your mother. I'll work out something. Promise me you won't tell her?"

"Why don't you want her to know?"

"I don't want her to come home because she thinks I'm in trouble. If she comes home it has to be because she wants to."

What he said didn't make sense to me. Why shouldn't she come home because he was in trouble and needed her? They always used to tell me to come to them if I was in trouble because that was what people close to you were for. Why do parents tell you one thing and do another? That is very confusing.

"Will you promise me?" Dad repeated.

"I suppose so, but I don't think it's right."

"This is something I have to decide, not you," Dad said. "Let's have some supper."

I went into the kitchen and opened a can of beans, heated them, and called him in for supper. "Is this our supper?" Dad asked.

"This is what people eat when they're poor," I told him.

Dad laughed, which was a good sign. "We can still eat, honey. I've got some money in savings."

"Well, I think we should practice and be prepared."

But Dad took some meat out of the refrig and made hamburgers, which I told him was very extravagant.

May

When you're in trouble everything happens at once. I no sooner think that nothing more can happen, when something else does. Today was a gorgeous spring day and in math class Roger handed me a note asking me to go for a walk with him after school. I was looking forward to it all day.

We met after school and headed for the park. Roger looked particularly handsome and I was glad I hadn't decided to give him up.

Roger was quieter than usual, but it was nice walking with him. I was quiet too, and the park was pretty with the trees budding and the grass all green. I felt good. Then Roger spoke in a serious voice. "I have something I want to say to you, but I don't know how to say it. I don't want to hurt your feelings."

My heart dropped at that. "My feelings don't get hurt easily," I lied gaily.

"I guess I'd better just come out with it. I'm not going to see you anymore. It's nothing against you," he spoke hurriedly as if he couldn't wait to get it all out. "But Millie and I have made an agreement not to go out with anyone else. I hope you don't mind."

I was stunned. "But Millie . . ." I almost told him the terrible things she said about him, but thank God I didn't. But Millie . . . that little hypocrite! I couldn't believe that anyone could lie to me so outrageously, I mean someone I knew, who was supposed to be my friend. If he had made an agreement (whatever the hell that is) with anyone else, I wouldn't have minded so much, but Millie!

"No, I don't mind," I lied again. And there we were in the middle of Central Park not knowing what to say to each other, and all I could think of was, my God, do I have to walk home with him? What do I do? I just wanted to run away. I never felt so stupid in my whole life.

"Millie and I are crazy about each other and so we promised not to see anyone else. Of course we'll see each other in school, and we can always be friends . . ."

123

He sounded like a pompous ass, and I wished he weren't so good looking and didn't make me feel so ridiculous.

"It's perfectly all right, Roger," I said to him. "I think I'd better go home. Thanks for telling me."

I turned around and started walking fast. When I finally got out of the park, I ran home. Coming into our empty apartment was the worst. But I didn't cry until I went into the bathroom and saw my face in the mirror. I had a smudge of chocolate on my chin (Roger had bought us pops) and the jerk hadn't even told me. I looked awful and then I cried, hating Roger for letting me walk around with a dirty face. I cried and cried. Only partly because of Roger, but a lot because Millie had betrayed me, my mother had betrayed me, and I had no one. No one at all.

I was really feeling sorry for myself. Roger was one of the things (persons) I couldn't talk to Grandma about. And I thought about how everybody lies, and if they don't lie outright, they never say what they mean or feel—the truth. I lied to Roger making believe I didn't care, Millie lied to me, my father is in a way lying to my mother by not telling her he'd like her to come home, she's lying to him by not admitting that she wants to. . . . I bet there's not a person in this whole world who doesn't tell lies, and the people who preach never to tell a lie are the biggest liars of all.

When I get terribly low, I often think about our house in Truro. It is the most beautiful place in the world and the best times I ever had in my life were spent there. I wished I could be there right now. I could walk on the beach, listen to the sea gulls, and find shells and crabs; maybe go out on the breakwater and pick mussels. When I went to bed at night I could listen to the water.

I thought so hard I almost felt that I was there. Then I got an idea.

End of May

I dread going home after school. If Dad is out,
I know he is looking for a job. Then I worry
about how he'll be when he comes home. I can
tell by the look on his face if he had a good inter-
view or a bad one. If he is home that's even
worse. He paces around the house trying to be
cheerful and making a total flop of it. He's also
taken to asking me a dozen times a day if I've
spoken to my mother. I wish she'd come home.

The idea I had is too wild to even think about.

I'm going down to see Mom tomorrow after
school. He made me promise again not to tell her
about his job but it's stupid not to.

June

I did something awful today. I don't know how or why I did it. Maybe I was possessed. Now I'm in such a mess I don't know what to do.

This is what happened: I went to see Mom and she looked terrible. As if she hadn't slept for days (I mean nights) and like she'd been crying. She asked me how Dad was. I said all right, but I must have said it funny.

"What's the matter?" she asked. "You're keeping something from me."

"I'm not keeping anything from you. Dad's okay."

"What do you mean 'okay'?"

"He misses you."

"I miss him, too." She looked at me and her eyes filled with tears. "I don't belong here, I'm miserable, and I can't go home now. I've ruined everything."

"Why can't you come home?" She was so unhappy she scared me. I felt a million years old. As if she was a child and I was her mother. But I didn't know how to be her mother, I felt that if I said or did the wrong thing I would ruin everything.

"I'm afraid to go home," she said. "I could go home and get into the same rut, and start hating myself again, feeling again that my life was being wasted . . ."

"But Dad needs you," I told her. "Listen . . ." and then the words came pouring out as if someone else was making me say them. I couldn't stop. "Dad quit his job and he's going up to Truro to paint," I lied. "He's going to be very lonesome up there without you. You could work on your piano while he paints."

She looked as if I'd hit her.

"I knew you were keeping something from me," she said. But she was still stunned. Then she started to cry for real. "After all these years," she sobbed. "At last he's doing what he always wanted to do, what I should have made him do from the beginning . . . now he's doing it without me . . ."

"He doesn't have to. You can be there with

him." I couldn't believe how much I was lying but I couldn't stop myself.

"What about you? You have to finish school. You couldn't live there."

"I could be there all summer. And I could stay with Grandma in the winter, and come up weekends. And Didi's not far away in Cambridge. Mom, it'll be fantastic."

"Does Dad plan to get free-lance design work until he can make money with his painting?"

"He hasn't talked about it." At least that wasn't a lie.

"I could probably get a job there in one of the shops—for the summer at least. That's what I'll do. I bet my friend Sophie, you know the one who makes that beautiful silver jewelry, would give me a job in her shop." Her face brightened, and then it fell. "I'm out of my mind," she said. "I don't know if he even wants me. Maybe I should call him."

"No, no, don't call him. Not yet." I was getting more and more hysterical.

She misunderstood me. "You're not telling me everything. He doesn't really want me, does he?"

"It's not that, Mom. It's that, well, I guess he wants to tell you himself about giving up his job and all . . ." I was getting in deeper and deeper. I couldn't say that I'd promised *not* to tell her. "Listen, I've got to go now. Don't do anything until you hear from me." I ran out before she could ask me any more questions.

She followed me to the door and said, "Sarah, you haven't told me anything about yourself, about school or anything . . ."

"I'll tell you later." I gave her a quick kiss and fled.

Outside I kept on running. I was scared stiff. But when I left her, she did look happier than when I'd arrived. That was something.

Later that evening

I'm a nervous wreck waiting for Dad to come home. What in the world am I going to tell him? That I'm a liar?

Later

Dear God, I didn't mean to do anything wrong. I just got a crazy idea (actually it sounded pretty sensible to me) and all I wanted to do was to say something to make Mom happy. Everyone tells lies, even me. I didn't mean to hurt anyone.

Dad came home and he wasn't quite so down as usual, so I thought I'd better tell him what happened. I was nervous, but I couldn't wait to get it off my chest so I blurted it right out. Before I could even tell him how excited she was, he let me have it.

He was furious. "What the hell do you think you're doing?" he screamed. "How can you make up such an outrageous lie? You're fooling around with people's lives—this is the maddest thing I ever heard of. You go right to the phone and tell your mother the truth!"

"But it made her so happy. She was so pleased and she *wants* to go up to Truro to live with you. She said she'd get a job in a shop so that you could paint. And that you could do free-lance design. She has it all figured out. I hate to tell her it's a lie."

Dad stared at me. "I don't care what she has figured out. I didn't quit my job, I got fired, and I've no intention of going up to Truro. You can't decide how people should run their lives. You go to that phone right now!"

"I'm not trying to run your life," I sobbed. "I didn't mean anything wrong. It was an idea I had and when I saw Mom looking so miserable, I told it to her. I don't care what you say, it is a good idea. You don't like it because you didn't think of it yourself. You're always like that—if you want to do something, everyone has to go, but if some-one else suggests it you always say you don't feel like it . . ."

"That's not true and don't use the word always."

"It is true, and it is always, I don't care."

"Listen, Sarah, I know this has been a rough time for you, but don't think you know every-thing. You're still a child, and a very fresh one right now."

"I'm not fresh, and I'm not a child. If I'm old enough to take care of myself, I'm old enough to have ideas. Just because I made this up doesn't make it wrong. Mom said you always wanted to paint, I don't see anything so crazy about it."

"You will not tell your mother and me how to live!"

"What difference does it make who has an idea, if it's good? Just because people get older doesn't make them smarter."

He made a motion to smack me but I ducked. "Don't you talk to me that way, you fresh kid."

"I'm not a kid," I yelled. "People don't stay kids forever. I've been taking care of myself all winter!"

I marched off to my room to write in my Diary. I did not call Mom.

The next day

I was nervous in school all day. First of all, Millie and Roger kept looking at me as if I cared that they were going together. I didn't, I had more important things on my mind. I should cross that out because that's another lie, and I want to tell only the truth here: I do mind. I wish I didn't have to see them every day. I hate the way they look at me. I honestly don't mind losing Roger but I hate the idea of them talking about me.

I wanted to tell Kathy what I did yesterday, but

it was too long and complicated. Besides it's hard to be completely honest.

It's like Grandma says, you build up defenses and you're afraid of sounding silly, and some things are too private to talk about. I couldn't tell anyone that I have long "thinks" about Adam, that I imagine him coming up to me and saying, "I fell in love with you the minute I saw you. I think about you all the time, but I never had the courage to tell you before . . ." That would be ridiculous because Adam would never talk that way and if he did it would never be to me.

I couldn't tell Grandma that sometimes I think my parents are stupid and that I wish I had different parents, more like Kathy's, although I don't know Mr. Stickney hardly at all. And I couldn't tell anyone what a disappointment Didi is to me —how I used to think that sometime, "when I got older," we'd be real close friends; but even though she was nice to me when I visited her and Eric I know that we're on different wave lengths. As far as Didi is concerned I'll never be a person but always a kid sister.

Of course I kept worrying all day about what was going to happen when I got home. I didn't see Dad before I left for school. He's usually up but he must have slept late, although he did call out good-bye to me. Maybe he was avoiding me. I prayed all day that we wouldn't have another row. I guess someone has to tell Mom the truth. I wish he would.

Late afternoon

I'm writing so much now I probably won't write in this again for months.

Dad was very preoccupied when I got home from school. He was at the kitchen table with the ashtray spilling over and a pad in front of him with a lot of figures. He pushed it away when I came in, like he didn't want me to see what he was doing.

"Hello," said I.

"I didn't realize it was so late." He seemed kind of embarrassed. I put my books on the table, naturally to see what he had on the paper. He was figuring out how much it would cost to live in Truro.

"They're just figures, Sarah. It doesn't change what you did, which was dead wrong. Have you called your mother?"

"No."

"You do it now and tell her the truth."

"I don't know what to say."

"You know damn well what to say. You tell her that you lied!"

"But what if we do go up to Truro to live? Then it won't be a lie."

"It's more than just a lie. It was a mischievous, meddling thing to do. Whatever we decide to do, *we'll* decide, your mother and I, and it won't change the fact that you lied."

I went into Didi's room; her phone was still there. I felt awful. I sat there trying to get up the courage to dial, hoping that my mother would be out. One of those women answered the phone, but she said my mother was there. I was as nervous as a cat. I blurted it out fast. "Forget what I said yesterday. I made it up. Dad didn't quit his job, he got fired. I made up the whole thing about his going up to Truro to paint. I'm sorry, Mom. It just happened, I didn't mean to do anything wrong. I thought it was a good idea."

There was a dead silence. "It's all right, Sarah. You're a good girl to tell me."

"I'm sorry, Mom . . ." I thought she was crying.

"It's okay. I'm sorry he lost his job. He probably wouldn't have wanted me to go with him anyway . . ."

When I hung up I was really bawling. Dad was standing in the doorway. I suppose he'd heard my end of the conversation, but I didn't care. "You're mean," I yelled. "It was a good idea—Mom thought so too. You're a stubborn pig not to do it."

Dad marched over to me and took my face in his hands. He has strong hands and he was pinching my cheeks. "Listen, Sarah, you can't go around arranging people's lives. Whether it's a good idea or not is beside the point. You'd better go and do your homework. I'm going out."

"Where are you going?"

"None of your business," he said. But I heard him go into the kitchen and dial the phone. I was positive he was calling Mom. He came back in a few minutes and said, "Can you fix your own dinner?"

"Of course."

"Okay. I won't be out late."

It was the longest evening I ever spent in my life. I almost called Grandma up, but I didn't. It was like I had to test myself to stay alone. It was hard, but I felt that if I didn't go crying for help, I wouldn't be a little kid anymore. It wasn't that I was afraid to stay alone, it was the agony of waiting, of knowing something important was happening, and that I had to be patient.

It was after ten when Dad came home. I was half asleep in front of the TV, exhausted from waiting.

"What happened?"

"What do you mean what happened?" Dad tried to look innocent.

"You saw Mom, didn't you?"

"Yes, I did."

"Are you going up to Truro?"

"You have a one-track mind. When I have anything to tell you I'll tell you. In the meantime you'd better go to bed."

I woke up enough to get mad. "Stop treating me like a baby. This concerns me as much as it does you. I'm sick of you and Mom not leveling with me. If you're going to be together I should know, and if you're going to get divorced I should know."

"Everything's not that simple. Maybe we don't know, ourselves. I bet you have private things you don't tell us. Some things you don't tell anyone, not even your own children."

"I'd tell you something important, like if I was going to get married."

"I would hope so, but your mother and I have

a lot of things to work out. You'll have to be patient."

"I'm sick of being patient," I mumbled, but I went to bed.

End of June

At last it's happened. I can't believe it. There were lots of meetings and phone calls and God knows what, and I had a nervous stomach for days, but we're really MOVING TO TRURO. It's hard to believe that only a few weeks ago everything was a mess. Mom says not to be fooled, that life doesn't stay fantastic, the way it is now.

It's wonderful having Mom home. She's busy getting rid of furniture and arranging things. She and Dad act a little peculiar wih each other, like they're both a little scared, and I guess maybe they are, but so far so good. I suppose Mom had to get that other stuff out of her system, and maybe it did help her. I get nervous when Dad teases her (which he does sometimes) about her loft, but she takes it okay, and comes right back at him saying it's always there if she wants to go back. But she is excited about the move and getting a job and Dad painting. Mom says you have to live through certain periods in your life and that each phase is a part of growing. I hope I'm in a phase now that lasts a long time because it's good.

July

The weirdest thing happened. Out of a clear sky I got a letter from Adam with a poem in it. He didn't write much (except for the poem) but he said he thought about me and wrote the poem. I don't know if I understand all the poem because it's about a deer who escapes from a wolf. I hope he thinks I'm the deer and not the wolf. The deer is very frightened, but brave and swift. I have a queer feeling that it's a warning to me not to get caught by someone or something evil. I wish I could talk to him about it. He wants me to write him a poem but I can't think of one.

Today I took Adam's poem (not that I needed it, I know it by heart) and went out on the breakwater, but all I could think of was his poem, not one of my own. I sat and looked at the water and didn't think of anything much except how good the sun felt.

Mom got her job and she was worried that I would be lonely. But I don't feel lonely. She asked if I wanted to invite a friend up to visit, but I don't think I do. I feel like being alone this summer. Mom looks at me with a worried expression—parents always want you to be doing something and they seem to think if you want to be alone there's something wrong. Mom and Dad are always busy. Mom works four days a week and Dad is painting and sometimes goes to New York to get free-lance work. He says we are poor now, and they think that makes me feel insecure. They couldn't be farther from the truth; I feel more secure than I ever have. I don't mind being poor, because we're not really poor. We have plenty to eat and a nice house, so what's poor about that? I don't mind not buying new clothes (I live in a bathing suit and shorts anyway) or not having a lot of furniture in the house—it's easier to clean this way. A dishwasher would be nice, but washing dishes is no big deal.

I wish I could think of a poem for Adam.

July

Didi and Eric are coming for the weekend.
Mom and Dad had a fight and that made me
nervous because I was afraid Mom would take
off again. Dad said he didn't see why they had to
condone her living with that boy and have him
for the weekend. Mom said that their living together was a fact, and it was stupid not to face it.
Besides she felt that they ought to get to know
Eric better. Mom won. I'm glad because I think
she is right, but they were both very cross for a
while.

Still July

I had a good time when Didi and Eric were here. Maybe I have to change my mind again about Didi—like Mom says, nothing ever stays the same. Not that we're ever going to be close friends, but she doesn't make me feel inferior anymore. I guess when you've been through as much as I have this past year, you come out stronger and more secure (if you survive). When she said my bathing suit was terrible, I didn't go into a tailspin. I laughed and said, "I like it," and that was that.

August

I wrote Adam a letter and told him that I couldn't write a poem but that I was going to write a story instead.

He wrote back right away and said that he hoped he could read it when I had it written. His letter made me feel good, like I was a real writer. So instead of writing in a diary I'm going to write a real story, maybe a whole book, I don't know. Everyone talks about writing instead of doing it so I'm not going to talk about it, but sit down and do it. So good-bye, Diary, at least for a while.

29778 · THE HOUSE OF THIRTY CATS, by Mary Calhoun. Illustrated by Mary Chalmers. Adventure and excitement enter Sarah's life when she pays her first visit to Miss Tabitha's wonderful house, meets the members of the cat community, and chooses a kitten of her very own. ($1.50)

29740 · THE TRUE STORY OF OKEE THE OTTER, by Dorothy Wisbeski. Illustrated with photographs. The beloved pet of a suburban family, Okee is a happy-go-lucky clown, curious about everything, and in and out of mischief. ($1.25)

29809 · ME AND THE TERRIBLE TWO, by Ellen Conford. Illustrated by Charles Carroll. When her best friend moves away, Dorrie is certain that she'll never be happy again—especially with those two impossible twin boys who moved in next door. ($1.25)

29509 · ALVIN FERNALD, MAYOR FOR A DAY, by Clifford B. Hicks. Illustrated by Bill Sokol. During his one-day administration, Alvin tackles the problems of Riverton and gets unexpected, hilarious results. (75¢)

29926